HI THERE, PUZZLE LOVERS!

JOIN ME (WALDO!) AND MY FRIENDS WOOF, WENDA, WIZARD WHITEBEARD, AND ODLAW FOR SOME TRICKY TEASERS AND PUZZLING PUZZLES.

THERE ARE ALL SORTS OF CHALLENGES BETWEEN THESE PAGES, AND EVEN A FOLDOUT BOARD GAME TO PLAY— WOW! YOU CAN TAKE THIS BOOK WITH YOU ANYWHERE: IN THE CAR, ON A TRAIN, A PLANE, OR IN A HOT AIR BALLOON . . . OR EVEN AT HOME ON THE SOFA!

STRETCH YOUR BRAIN TO ITS LIMITS WITH THESE MIND-BOGGLING GAMES AND OTHER INCREDIBLE THINGS TO FIND AND DO ALONG THE WAY.

DON'T FORGET TO KEEP AN EYE OUT FOR THE
WALDO-WATCHERS. THEY COULD APPEAR AT ANY TIME!

PLUS PLENTY OF MY OLD PALS ARE WANDERING
BETWEEN THE SCENES, SO STAY ALERT!

SOME SEARCHES AREN'T AS SIMPLE AS THEY
FIRST APPEAR, AND SOME CODES ARE MORE CRACKABLE
THAN YOU MIGHT THINK, BUT ALL THE PUZZLES, GAMES,
AND BRAIN-BUSTERS ARE FANTASTICALLY FUN! THERE ARE
ANSWERS TO SOME OF THE PUZZLES AT THE END OF
THE BOOK. SO GO ALONE OR INVITE SOME FRIENDS
TO HELP YOU, AND LET THE JOURNEY BEGIN!

Waldo

HI THERE, WALDO FANS!

I'M OFF ON ANOTHER ADVENTURE, AND YOU CAN COME TOO! BUT WATCH OUT! THERE ARE SOME PERPLEXING, PRACTICALLY IMPOSSIBLE PUZZLES IN THIS POCKET-SIZE COMPENDIUM! WOOF, WIZARD WHITEBEARD, WENDA, ODLAW, AND I HAVE COME ACROSS ALL SORTS OF MANIC MAYHEM ON OUR TRAVELS, AND IT'S UP TO YOU TO HELP US OUT. IT'S MY TURN FIRST! CAN YOU CRACK THIS SELECTION OF WACKY WORD PUZZLES, SILLY SEARCHES, AND OTHER TOPSY-TURVY TRICKS? GOOD LUCK!

Waldo

TRAVEL ESSENTIALS

Waldo is about to set off on his travels.
Check off everything he's carrying from the list
below, and then find the objects he's missing
in the scene behind him. Bon voyage!

BACKPACK
BALLOON
BELT
BINOCULARS
BUCKET
CAMERA
CLOCK
CUP
FLOWER
MALLET
POM-POM

SATCHEL
SHOVEL
SLEEPING BAG
SNORKEL
SPINNING TOP
TEAPOT
TOP HAT
WALKING STICK

MORE THINGS TO DO

There are some things Waldo can't travel with! Unscramble the letters below to find out what he's leaving behind!

cera rac   Clue: vroom, vroom

dgrna iapno   Clue: musical keys

ckhneti snki   Clue: wash the dishes

HALL OF MIRRORS

In one of these mirrors, Waldo is facing in
the opposite direction from the way he's facing in
the other three. Can you spot which one?

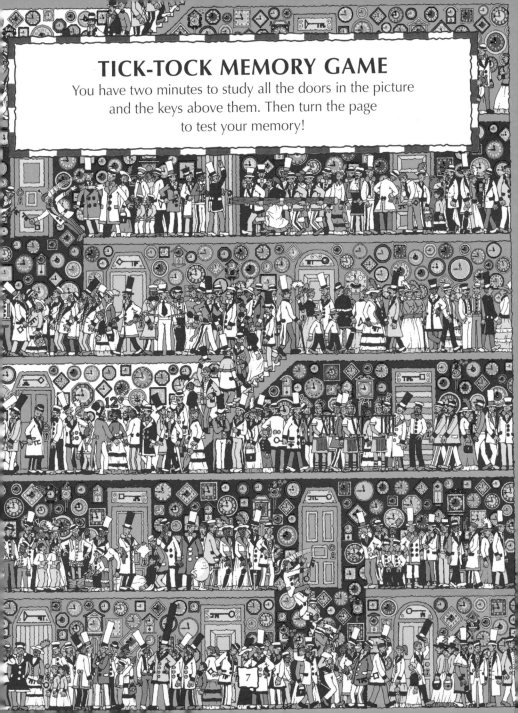

TICK-TOCK MEMORY GAME

You have two minutes to study all the doors in the picture and the keys above them. Then turn the page to test your memory!

TICK-TOCK MEMORY GAME

Can you remember which key goes above which door?
Draw a line from each key to the door it opens.

THROUGH THE KEYHOLE GAME

Take your time peeking through these keyholes.
Then turn back the page and find each section in the scene.

PYRAMID PUZZLE

Search for the words at the bottom of this page in the pyramid puzzle.
The words go up, down, forward, and backward.

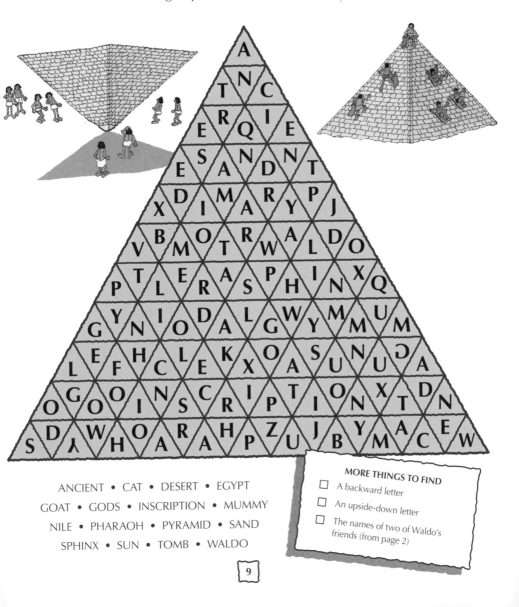

ANCIENT • CAT • DESERT • EGYPT
GOAT • GODS • INSCRIPTION • MUMMY
NILE • PHARAOH • PYRAMID • SAND
SPHINX • SUN • TOMB • WALDO

MORE THINGS TO FIND
☐ A backward letter
☐ An upside-down letter
☐ The names of two of Waldo's friends (from page 2)

WILD AND WACKY *W*'S

Can you fit all of the *W* words in the puzzle? One of the words has *wandered* backward, and another doesn't begin with *W* but is *all over*.

WAHOO

WAVE

WHOOPEE

WHOOSH

WONDER

EVERYWHER

WHIZZ

WEB

WILD

WITTY

WIG

WO...

WISE

REDNAW

WAVE

WACKY

MORE THINGS TO DO

How quickly can you say this tongue-twister? Waldo wishes Wenda would wear a water-proof watch!

BALLOON BEDLAM

What a terrific tangle! Follow the strings to find out which balloons Waldo and his friends are holding.

MORE THINGS TO DO

Look at the patterns in the border to find a sequence that matches the order of the patterns on the balloons. Then color in the pattern on the empty balloon.

STARS AND STRIPES

Which path leads from Waldo's seal to the golden star? You better hurry, because there are multiple Waldos trying to reach it!

MORE THINGS TO FIND

☐ A striped walking stick

☐ A hat with a blue pom-pom

FUNNY FACE FLAGS

What a frenzied flurry of fierce and funny flags! Can you find these eleven foolish faces in the scene below?

MORE THINGS TO FIND

☐ Two snakes

☐ A game of tic-tac-toe

☐ Ten milk bottles

13

TERRIFIC TRAVELS

Study the pictures of the extraordinary lands
Waldo has visited. How many of each item
listed next to each picture can you find?

Red birds:

Pies thrown:

Green hoods:

Pairs of sunglasses:

Hats with feathers:

Yellow fish:

Mustaches:

MORE THINGS TO FIND

☐ Waldo's spare pair of glasses

☐ A red and yellow feather

☐ Odlaw in a Waldo hat

14

PHEW! WHAT A WILD RIDE THAT WAS. YOU'RE A REAL BRAINIAC IF YOU BEAT THOSE BEFUDDLING FLIGHTS OF FANCY! BUT DON'T TAKE OFF YOUR THINKING CAPS YET—WE STILL HAVE A LONG WAY TO GO ON OUR JOURNEY. CARRY ON, WALDO-WATCHERS!

Can you find where these pictures come from in Waldo's chapter? But beware, there is one picture from elsewhere in the book!

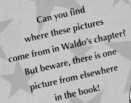

WALDO'S CHECKLIST

Wait, there's more! Look back over Waldo's journey and find . . .

☐ A clown with a cone-shaped head

☐ A Roman clock

☐ Three people talking on walkie-talkies

☐ A soldier with a white beard

☐ Two clocks with smiling faces

☐ Two clowns sharing a hat

☐ An egg timer

☐ A set of tea-shirts

☐ A cake with nine candles

☐ A dog wearing sunglasses

☐ People sliding on mats

ONE LAST THING . . .

Can you find Waldo's key hidden somewhere in this section? Keep your eyes peeled—there are some trick keys out there!

BOWWOW!

RUFF, RUFF! WOOF HERE! ARE YOU READY FOR SOME TAIL-WAGGINGLY GOOD GAMES? MY POOCH PALS AND I HAVE BEEN REALLY PUZZLING OVER THE CHALLENGES AHEAD, AND WE'RE HOPING YOU CAN HELP US OUT. THERE ARE PLENTY OF ANSWERS FOR YOU TO SNIFF OUT, SO TAKE THE LEAD AND FOLLOW ME THROUGH THESE CRAZY CANINE CONUNDRUMS. GOOD LUCK!

BARE BONES BRAIN BUSTER
Take your time to study this scene closely.
Then turn the page to test your memory.

BARE BONES BRAIN BUSTER

How many of these questions can you answer from memory?
(It's also fun to guess!) Then turn back the page to see how you did.

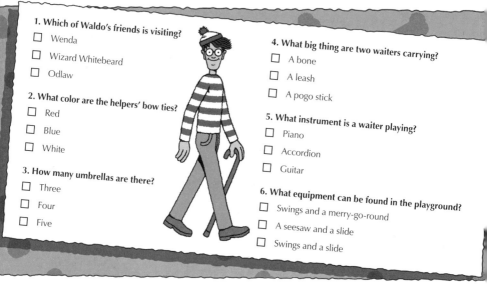

1. Which of Waldo's friends is visiting?
- ☐ Wenda
- ☐ Wizard Whitebeard
- ☐ Odlaw

2. What color are the helpers' bow ties?
- ☐ Red
- ☐ Blue
- ☐ White

3. How many umbrellas are there?
- ☐ Three
- ☐ Four
- ☐ Five

4. What big thing are two waiters carrying?
- ☐ A bone
- ☐ A leash
- ☐ A pogo stick

5. What instrument is a waiter playing?
- ☐ Piano
- ☐ Accordion
- ☐ Guitar

6. What equipment can be found in the playground?
- ☐ Swings and a merry-go-round
- ☐ A seesaw and a slide
- ☐ Swings and a slide

EXTRA BONE-OCULAR EYE-BOGGLER

Study these close-ups carefully and turn back the page to find them.

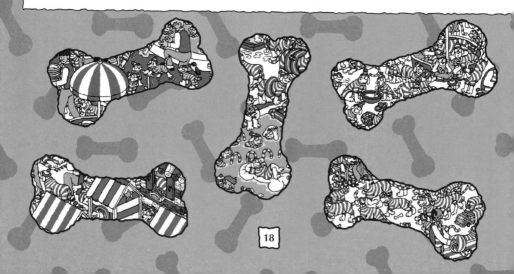

TO THE TAIL END

Find a way through the maze of Woof tails. Start at the square with the red tail and use the guide below to help you reach the square with the white tail.

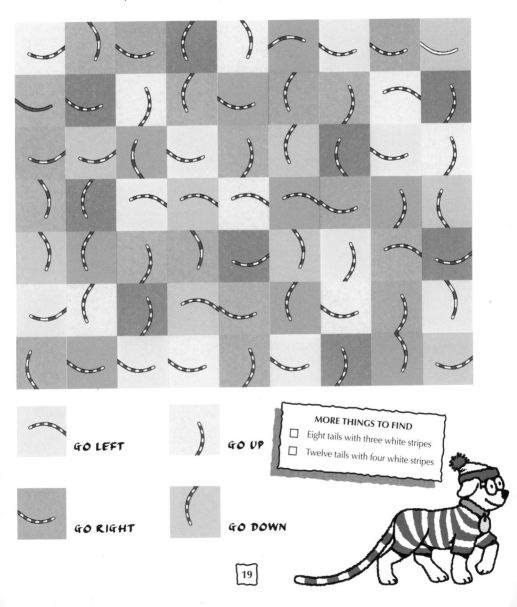

GO LEFT

GO UP

GO RIGHT

GO DOWN

MORE THINGS TO FIND
- ☐ Eight tails with three white stripes
- ☐ Twelve tails with four white stripes

WHO'S WHO?

What a mix-up! Unscramble the anagrams and fill in the boxes next to them. Then draw a line to match the pictures to your answers.

OWOF	
GIMNCIAA	
DALWO	
LDOWA AWCTERH	
VEMCANA	
IPARET	
RIOSNDAU	
CTAROAB	
IGHNKT	
GIKINV	

MORE THINGS TO DO

Write an anagram of your name in the empty space!

WOOF'S WORD WHEEL

Use the clues to help you find five words using three or more letters in the word wheel. Each answer must contain the letter *O* only once.

CLUES

1. It's as hard as rock.
2. Woof's favorite thing
3. Used to sniff
4. Heads, shoulders, knees, and . . .
5. Woof is one of these.

2.

3.

4.

5.

MORE THINGS TO DO
See how many other words you can make using the word wheel.

TRUTH OR TAILS?

Test your knowledge of Woof's ancient four-legged friends and work out which statements are true and which are false.

1. The word dinosaur means "terrible lizard."

2. A dinosaur scientist is called a dinotologist.

3. Dinosaurs laid eggs.

4. This anagram spells a dinosaur's name: RETTSRIPOCA

5. A tyrannosaurus's bite was roughly three times stronger than that of a lion.

6. The ankylosaurus had a club tail.

7. The dinosaur with the longest name is a micropachycephalosaurus.

8. A pterodactyl had three wings.

9. A brachiosaurus had a very short neck.

10. The dinosaurs lived until sixty-five thousand years ago.

Use the Internet or an encyclopedia to look up more fun facts about dinosaurs!

DID YOU KNOW?

There was a dinosaur similar to a dog! It is called Cynognathus (*sy-nog-nay-thus*) and was a hairy mammal-like animal with dog-like teeth. Woof claims that his great-great-great-grandfather was one (calculated in dog years, of course)!

ONE MORE THING!

What is the name of the dinosaur whose skeleton is in this picture? *Clue: it begins with the letter S.*

DOG'S DINNER

Cross out all the *W*'s to decode Woof's message.
Write the answer in the spaces below each line.
Two *W*'s means a break between words.

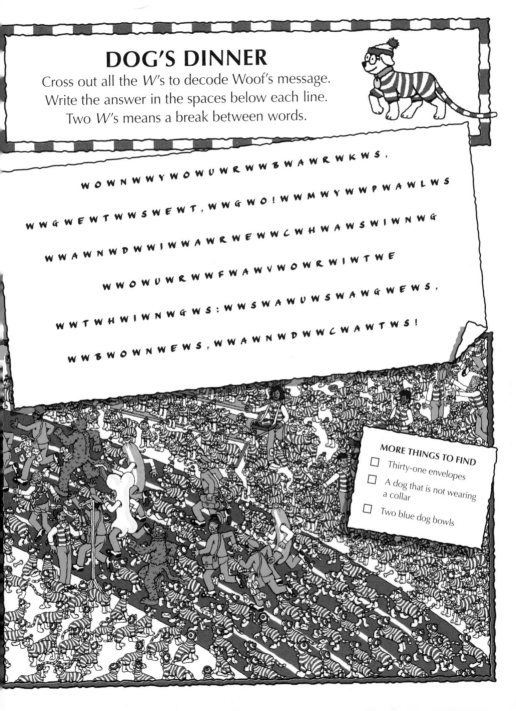

W O W N W W Y W O W U W R W W B W A W R W K W S ,

W W G W E W T W W S W E W T , W W G W O ! W W M W Y W W P W A W L W S

W W A W N W D W W I W W A W R W E W W C W H W A W S W I W N W N W G

W W O W U W R W W F W A W V W O W R W I W T W E

W W T W H W I W N W G W S : W W S W A W U W S W A W G W E W S ,

W W B W O W N W E W S , W W A W N W D W W C W A W T W S !

MORE THINGS TO FIND

☐ Thirty-one envelopes

☐ A dog that is not wearing a collar

☐ Two blue dog bowls

BURIED BONES

Woof has been busy burying bones! Can you fill in
the grid coordinates for the items at the bottom of
the page to mark where he has hidden them?

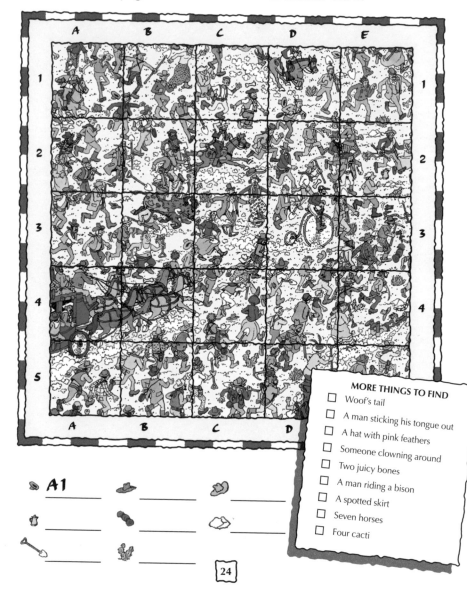

MORE THINGS TO FIND
- ☐ Woof's tail
- ☐ A man sticking his tongue out
- ☐ A hat with pink feathers
- ☐ Someone clowning around
- ☐ Two juicy bones
- ☐ A man riding a bison
- ☐ A spotted skirt
- ☐ Seven horses
- ☐ Four cacti

A1 _____ _____ _____

_____ _____ _____

_____ _____

RUFF, RUFF! YOU'RE CERTAINLY NO BONEHEAD! THANKS FOR HELPING ME AND MY POOCH PALS PICK APART THESE PUZZLES. WE LIKE TO KEEP YOU ON YOUR PAWS, SO KEEP GOING FOR MORE FUN AND GAMES!

PLUS THERE ARE MORE PUPPY PUZZLES BELOW!

Can you spot these pictures somewhere in Woof's chapter? But hold your horses, one picture is from a different place entirely!

WOOF'S CHECKLIST

Pad back through Woof's wonderful wanders and find . . .

- ☐ Seven red dog bowls
- ☐ A watch dog
- ☐ An old-fashioned bicycle
- ☐ A sand castle
- ☐ A falling tree
- ☐ Sherlock Woof
- ☐ A man being poked by a spear
- ☐ A cat dressed as Woof
- ☐ A rubber duck
- ☐ A woman wearing a fur coat
- ☐ A bluebird wearing a pom-pom hat

ONE LAST THING . . .

Can you find Woof's bone in this section? Don't be fooled by any fake bones!

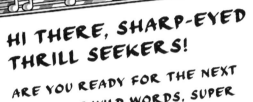

HI THERE, SHARP-EYED THRILL SEEKERS!

ARE YOU READY FOR THE NEXT ROUND OF WILD WORDS, SUPER SEARCHES, AND BRILLIANT BRAIN GAMES? IT'S BEEN A CRAZY JOURNEY SO FAR, BUT NOW IS YOUR CHANCE TO TAKE ON SOME REAL CHALLENGES. THERE'S LOTS OF CAMERA CHAOS AND MUSICAL MAYHEM ON THE PAGES AHEAD, SO STAY SHARP!

GOOD LUCK, ADVENTURERS!

SNAPPY SINGING!

These stamping feet are creating cracks everywhere in this spectacular singing scene. Can you find the seven broken things from the list below?

BROKEN THINGS TO FIND
- ☐ A smashed mirror
- ☐ Woof's snapped bone
- ☐ A bent umbrella
- ☐ A split stage
- ☐ A broken walking stick
- ☐ A ladder with a broken rung
- ☐ Wenda's broken glasses

A COLORFUL TUNE

Can you find these sets of musical notes inside the grid?
The answers run across, down, and diagonally.

MORE THINGS TO FIND

- ☐ A man looking through a porthole
- ☐ A backward note in the grid
- ☐ Ten musical T-shirts
- ☐ Five trumpets
- ☐ A man in a drum

BUSY BANDSTAND

What a musical muddle! Look at the clapper board and match up the instruments with the items or pieces used to play them.

DRUM	
CLARINET	MOUTHPIECE
GUITAR	BOW
TROMBONE	KEYS
VIOLIN	ROD
TRIANGLE	PICK
PIANO	REED
	STICKS

29

MORE THINGS TO DO
* Find animal costumes in the scene beginning with the letters B, C, P, and R.
* Sing your favorite song!

UNDER THE SPOTLIGHT

Lights, camera, action! Can you spot ten differences between these two musical stage scenes?

MORE THINGS TO DO

Create your own checklist of things to find in the scenes.

- ☐ ....
- ☐ ....
- ☐ ....
- ☐ ....
- ☐ ....
- ☐ ....

LOST LUGGAGE

Spot Wenda's lost luggage in these photographs.
Can you find one bag with a red-and-white-striped luggage label,
two bags with white labels, and two bags with blue labels?

MORE THINGS TO FIND

- [ ] A bag with a red luggage label
- [ ] A woman wearing yellow shoes
- [ ] A barrel
- [ ] Seven yellow luggage labels

31

CAKE-TASTROPHE!

Help Wenda figure out all the ingredients for this cake recipe by crossing out the letters in gray that spell *Wenda* in every word.

WSEUGNADRA

WBEUNTTDEAR

EWGENGDAS

FWLENODAUR

VWANEILLNA EDXTRAACT

BWAEKING NPODWDAER

MORE THINGS TO FIND

- ☐ A gingerbread person
- ☐ Wenda's cake with three red layers
- ☐ A double-ended wooden spoon

32

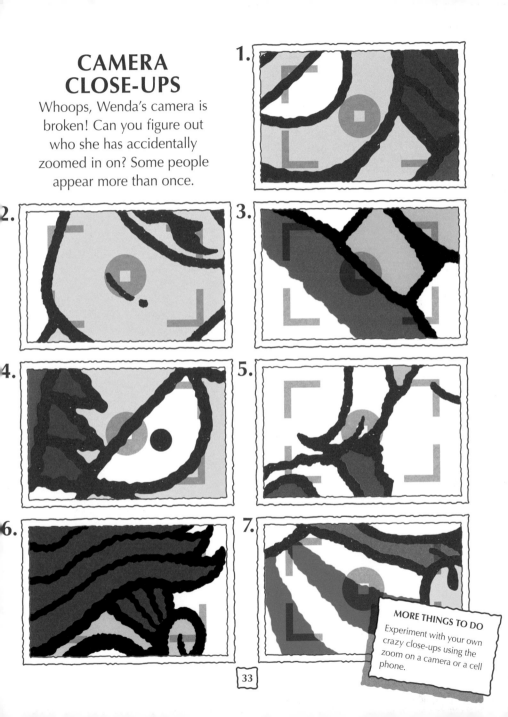

CAMERA CLOSE-UPS

Whoops, Wenda's camera is broken! Can you figure out who she has accidentally zoomed in on? Some people appear more than once.

1.

2.

3.

4.

5.

6.

7.

MORE THINGS TO DO

Experiment with your own crazy close-ups using the zoom on a camera or a cell phone.

MUSICAL FRAME FUN

Wenda has framed her favorite musical photographs. Can you find a picture that doesn't contain a musical note and one with Wenda's face in the frame?

MORE THINGS TO FIND
- [ ] Twelve violins
- [ ] A large bow tie
- [ ] A guitar
- [ ] Three tubas
- [ ] A one-eyed man

DANCING SILHOUETTES

Wenda has sent you a postcard from her party. Match the silhouettes with her funky-stepping friends on the dance floor.

I'M HAVING SUCH A GREAT TIME PLAYING MY FAVORITE TUNES, AND LOTS OF PEOPLE ARE BUSTING THEIR BEST MOVES ON THE DANCE FLOOR! HERE ARE THE BEST ONES SO FAR . . .

WENDA

MORE THINGS TO FIND

Five letters are hidden in this scene that spell out Wenda's favorite dance.

Clue: the word starts with the first letter of her name.

_ _ _ _ _

WOBBLY WORD LADDERS

Hang on! Can you fill in the missing words in these ladders? Start at the top and work your way down by changing one letter at a time but keeping the rest of the letters in the same order.

HAT

_ _ _

_ _ _

_ _ _

KEY

MALT

_ _ _ _

_ _ _ _

_ _ _ _

GAME

MORE THINGS TO FIND
- [ ] A hat with a red pom-pom
- [ ] A parrot
- [ ] A football player

WOW! WHAT A SAVVY SEARCHER YOU ARE! DID YOU FIND IT TOUGH TACKLING ALL THOSE SCRAMBLED SCENES AND WACKY WORDS? I HOPE IT WASN'T TOO TRICKY. THERE ARE STILL SOME MIND-BOGGLERS FOR YOU TO BATTLE WITH, SO KEEP GOING!

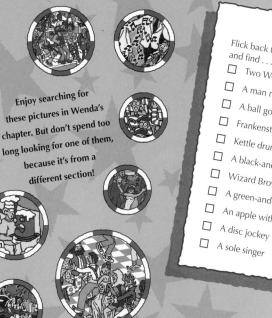

Enjoy searching for these pictures in Wenda's chapter. But don't spend too long looking for one of them, because it's from a different section!

WENDA'S CHECKLIST

Flick back through Wenda's extravaganza and find . . .

☐ Two Wendas wearing blue shoes

☐ A man napping in a piano

☐ A ball gown

☐ Frankenstein's monster

☐ Kettle drums

☐ A black-and-yellow luggage label

☐ Wizard Brownbeard

☐ A green-and-white-striped umbrella

☐ An apple with a pie

☐ A disc jockey

☐ A sole singer

ONE LAST THING . . .

Did you spot Wenda's camera? Only one is picture-perfect. The others are fake, so be on the lookout!

GREETINGS, BRAVE ADVENTURERS!

HOW WISE YOU MUST BE TO HAVE MADE IT THIS FAR! BUT BEWARE, THE PATH AHEAD IS MISTED BY ALL SORTS OF MANIC MAZES, MIX-UPS, AND MYSTERIES. CAN YOU USE YOUR WISDOM TO WORK THROUGH THIS WIZARDRY, OR WILL IT LEAVE YOU UTTERLY BAMBOOZLED AND BEWITCHED?

FAREWELL FOR NOW.

WORD CASTLE

Find the words at the bottom of this page in the three-letter bricks of this castle. A word can read across more than one brick.

R	O	F		A	Q	U	E	E	N		A	O	E
M	X	A		J	O	P	W	W	O		W	G	R
L	W	A	D	R	A	W	B	R	I	D	G	E	H	L	D	R	A
O	A	R	M	O	R	U	E	K	R	C	A	T	A	P	U	L	T
N	T	P	C	A	S	T	L	E	L	Q	P	U	F	M	P	X	E
W	Q	L	E	U	H	E	L	M	E	T	A	B	A	T	T	L	E
M	O	A	T	H	Y	K	W	S	E	M	I	U	L	E	I	A	F
D	G	E	M	I	L	A	I	N	S	I	S	W	O	R	D	W	R
A	R	R	O	W	H	R	E	E	A	K	L	K	C	E	T	L	H
H	F	M	A	R	A	W	N	P	M	T	L	H	F	L	A	G	T
W	K	I	N	G	O	H	Y	O	E	A	B	C	R	O	W	N	G

MORE THINGS TO DO

Work out the two magic words that can open the castle drawbridge. Then find it hidden in the word castle!

Hint: the letters go up, across, and down.

O _ _ _ / _ _ S _ _ E

WORDS TO FIND

ARMOR
ARROW
BATTLE
CASTLE
CATAPULT
CROWN
DRAWBRIDGE
HELMET
KING
MOAT
QUEEN
SWORD

MIX-UP MADNESS

What a muddle! Match the top halves of these characters to the correct bottom halves.

GIANT GAME

Start on the board game square next to each player's picture.
Then follow each footstep guide to work out who picks up the scroll.

MORE THINGS TO FIND

☐ Nine men wearing helmets

☐ Someone wearing blue-and-yellow tights

☐ Four pitchforks

SOMETHING FISHY

Match up the sets of three identically colored fish. One fish is not part of a set, so have a splish-splashing time finding out which one!

MORE THINGS TO FIND

☐ A smiling fish

☐ An angry fish

☐ A fish with closed eyes

TELEPORTATION TANGLE

What a tangle! Follow the teleportation rays to find out who's traveling where.

MORE THINGS TO DO
How many books is Waldo holding? What do you think they're about?

SHIELDS AND STAVES

En garde —eyes at the ready! Find two pictures that are the same.

MORE THINGS TO FIND

☐ Four blue shields

☐ Eight green hats

☐ A carved red staff

☐ A man with stars above his head

GENIE-OUS!

Draw in the missing symbols to release the genie from its lamp! All nine symbols must appear once in each box, but never in the same row or column.

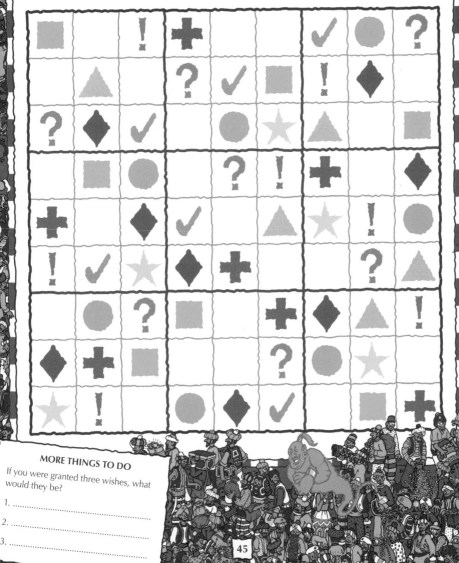

MORE THINGS TO DO

If you were granted three wishes, what would they be?

1. ....

2. ....

3. ....

DOUBLE VISION

All is not what it seems with these magic monks and red-cloaked ghouls.
Spot six differences between these two scenes.

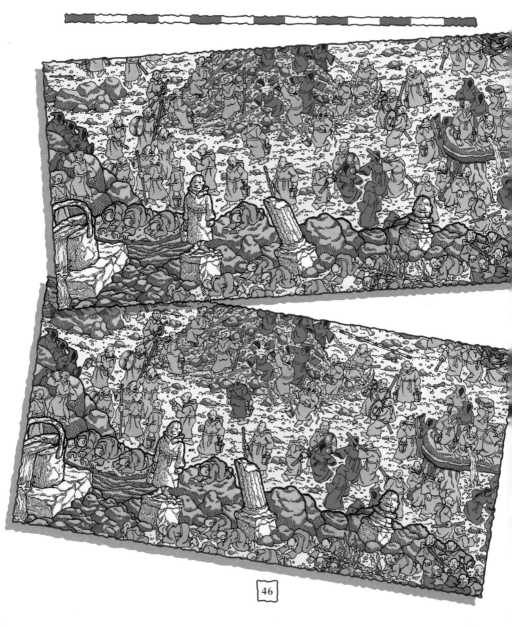

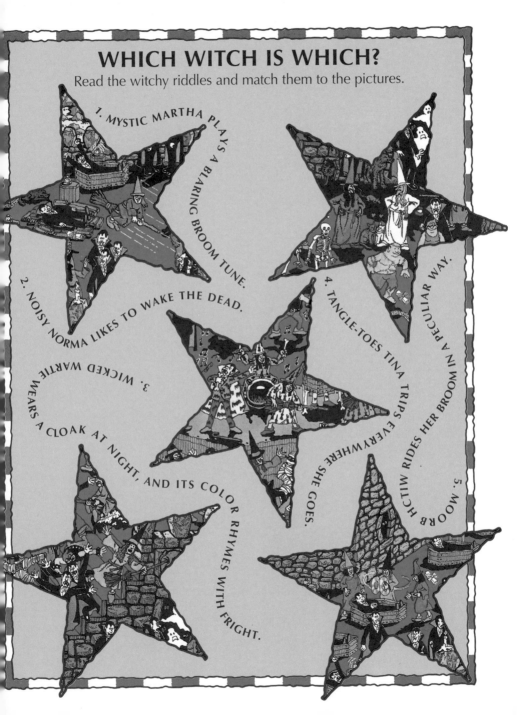

WHICH WITCH IS WHICH?
Read the witchy riddles and match them to the pictures.

1. MYSTIC MARTHA PLAYS A BLARING BROOM TUNE.

2. NOISY NORMA LIKES TO WAKE THE DEAD.

3. WICKED WARTIE WEARS A CLOAK AT NIGHT, AND ITS COLOR RHYMES WITH FRIGHT.

4. TANGLE-TOES TINA TRIPS EVERYWHERE SHE GOES.

5. WOBBLY WITCH RIDES HER BROOM IN A PECULIAR WAY.

WISE CRACKS

Wizard Whitebeard has cast a happy spell!
This scroll is inscribed with lots of jokes.
Which one makes you laugh the most?

HOW DO WIZARDS SET THE
TABLE FOR A TEA PARTY?

WITH CUPS AND
FLYING SORCERERS!

MORE THINGS TO DO
Make up your own
joke and write it in the
space on the scroll!

HOW MANY WIZARDS DOES IT TAKE
TO CAST A SPELL OF INVISIBILITY?

I DON'T KNOW, I CAN'T SEE THEM!

HOW CAN YOU DESCRIBE
A WIZARD'S BOOK?

SPELL-BINDING!

WHY CAN'T WIZARDS
CLEAN FLOORS?

BECAUSE THE WITCHES
STOLE THEIR BROOMS!

WHAT DID THE MAGICIAN DO
WHEN HE WAS VERY ANGRY?

HE PULLED HIS HARE OUT!

....

....

....

BLESS MY BEARD, YOU HAVE A TRULY MAGICAL MIND! CONGRATULATIONS ON WORKING THROUGH MY SILLY SORCERY. YOU'RE NEARLY AT THE END OF THIS TRICKSY PATH OF PUZZLES AND PANDEMONIUM, BUT THERE ARE STILL PLENTY OF TESTS ON THIS QUIZZICAL QUEST. I WISH YOU THE VERY BEST OF LUCK.

WIZARD WHITEBEARD'S SCROLL CHECKLIST

Cast your eyes over Wizard Whitebeard's quest and find . . .

- ☐ Wizard Whitebeard in a boat
- ☐ A sea lion
- ☐ A windmill
- ☐ Four jumping fish
- ☐ A gargoyle breathing fire
- ☐ Three genies
- ☐ A man who has gone through a shield
- ☐ A wishing well
- ☐ A skeleton
- ☐ A minstrel with a terrible singing voice
- ☐ Two cats in love

Can you spot these scenes from Wizard Whitebeard's section? But riddle me this — one of them comes from somewhere else in the book!

ONE LAST THING . . .

Have you spotted Wizard Whitebeard's scroll somewhere in this section? Only the scroll with the red bow contains the right magic spell.

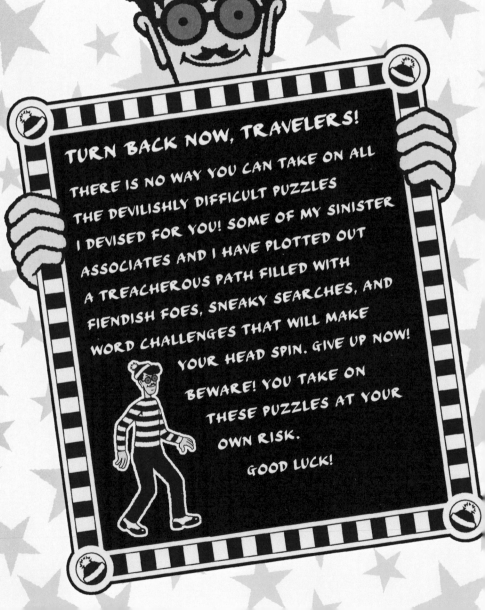

TURN BACK NOW, TRAVELERS!
THERE IS NO WAY YOU CAN TAKE ON ALL THE DEVILISHLY DIFFICULT PUZZLES I DEVISED FOR YOU! SOME OF MY SINISTER ASSOCIATES AND I HAVE PLOTTED OUT A TREACHEROUS PATH FILLED WITH FIENDISH FOES, SNEAKY SEARCHES, AND WORD CHALLENGES THAT WILL MAKE YOUR HEAD SPIN. GIVE UP NOW! BEWARE! YOU TAKE ON THESE PUZZLES AT YOUR OWN RISK.
GOOD LUCK!

DISGUISE, DISGUISE!

Oh, no! Here are twelve Odlaws. But which is the real one? Figure it out as quickly as possible!

ORE THINGS TO DO
Color in the Odlaws!

Spot something wrong with the pattern on the frame!

TOP FIENDS

Meet Odlaw's most ferocious team of fiends. Look at the pictures on the cards and match them to the correct description.

Name: Hungry Growler
Home: Swamp
Favorite Food: Everything and anything
Speed: Lumbering
Courage: 10
Spy Ability: 2
Fear Factor: 8
Special Skill: Roaring and emitting foul smells

Name: Heave-Ho Henry
Home: Dungeon
Favorite Food: Nuts and bolts
Speed: Slow when rusty
Courage: 4
Spy Ability: 9
Fear Factor: 10
Special Skill: Sneaking up on people

Name: Captain Cutlass
Home: The Black Skull
Favorite Food: Dried meats
Speed: Peg-leg slow
Courage: 9
Spy Ability: 6
Fear Factor: 6
Special Skill: Pillaging

Name: Warty Gretel
Home: The Witch's Castle
Favorite Food: Bats' tails, frogs' legs, eyes of a newt
Speed: Fast on a broom
Courage: 4
Spy Ability: 10
Fear Factor: 6
Special Skill: Potions and curses

MORE THINGS TO DO

* Who ranks the highest for their spying skills?
* Who is the most courageous?
* Who is the most terrifying?

SUPER-SNEAKY SEA-GAZING GAME

Odlaw loves to look out to sea with his pirate friends. Study the scene closely and find everything noted in the ship's logbook below.

- ☐ Three men wearing skull-and-crossbones T-shirts
- ☐ Two hats with green feathers
- ☐ Three men with yellow beards
- ☐ Four men wearing red-and-white striped pants
- ☐ Three men wearing yellow bandanas with black spots
- ☐ Five flying swords

SUPER-SNEAKY SEA-GAZING GAME

How closely did you study Odlaw's pirate scene? Look through these binocular views and find them on the previous page.

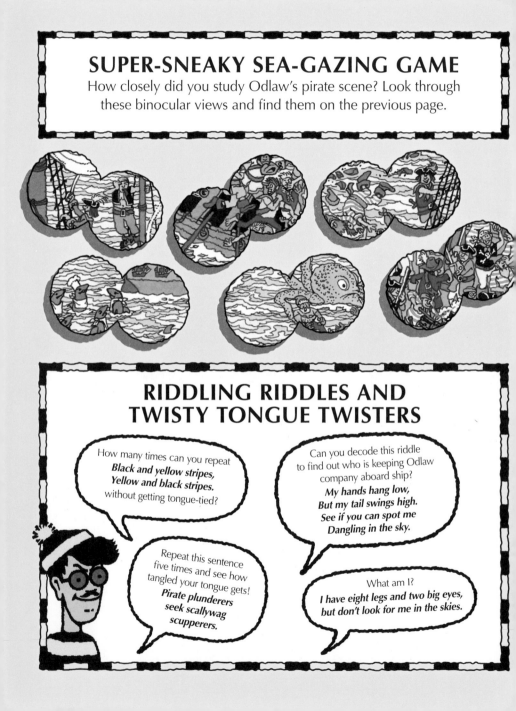

RIDDLING RIDDLES AND TWISTY TONGUE TWISTERS

How many times can you repeat
Black and yellow stripes,
Yellow and black stripes.
without getting tongue-tied?

Can you decode this riddle to find out who is keeping Odlaw company aboard ship?
My hands hang low,
But my tail swings high.
See if you can spot me
Dangling in the sky.

Repeat this sentence five times and see how tangled your tongue gets!
Pirate plunderers
seek scallywag
scupperers.

What am I?
I have eight legs and two big eyes,
but don't look for me in the skies.

MONOCHROME MONSTERS

Color in this monstrous tower
scene with your wackiest colors!

MORE THINGS TO FIND

- [ ] Seven spotted dragons
- [ ] Nine ladders
- [ ] A dragon flying upside down
- [ ] A sailor in striped clothes
- [ ] A dragon wearing flying goggles

55

SNAKING WORDS

Read the clues and work out the answers by connecting the letters inside each frame without taking your pen off the paper!

1. Clue: A sea-traveling invader

N I
G K
V I

2. Clue: A sword-swishing soldier

E   T E
K M E
S U R

3. Clue: A skeletal symbol used by pirates

K S S E B S
U A N N O S
L L D C R O

MORE THINGS TO FIND

☐ Nine yellow-headed birds
☐ Three vampires
☐ A flying witch

PIRATEY PUZZLE

Ahoy there! Fill in the answers next to these questions to reveal a word going downward that is Odlaw's favorite part of a piratey disguise!

The __ seas (*clue: number of days in a week*)

Observing in secret

The rear part of a ship

Person in charge of the ship and its crew

Odlaw's treasure-hunting shipmates

Message in a _____

A heavy weight on rope that keeps a ship in one place

Pieces of __ (*clue: a number between 7 and 9*)

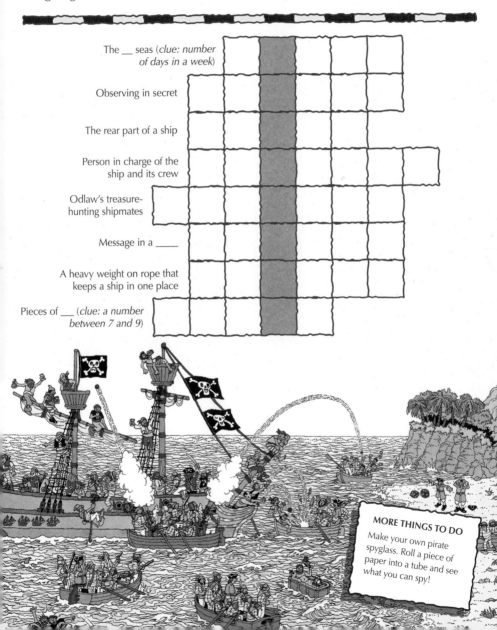

MORE THINGS TO DO

Make your own pirate spyglass. Roll a piece of paper into a tube and see what you can spy!

SLIPPERY SEARCH

Using your finger, trace a path through the tunnels to help Odlaw escape and pick up his slithery black-and-yellow-striped companion on the way.

58

WELL, WELL, WELL . . . THIS IS A SURPRISE. CONGRATULATIONS, YOU'RE ALMOST AS CUNNING AS I AM. MAYBE NEXT TIME YOU CAN JOIN ME ON MY QUEST TO FOIL WALDO. BUT FOR NOW, THERE ARE STILL SOME THINGS FOR YOU TO FIND! DID YOU REALLY THINK IT WAS GOING TO BE THAT EASY? GOOD LUCK, I SUPPOSE.

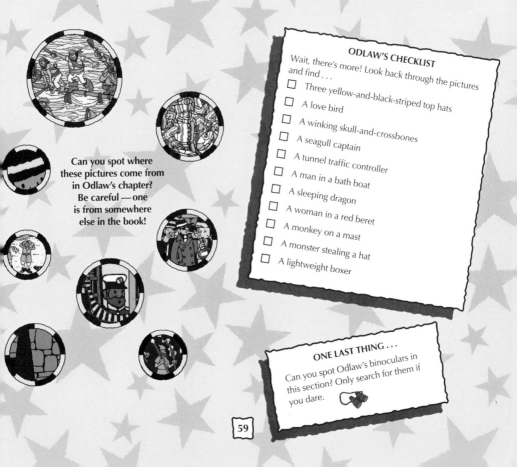

Can you spot where these pictures come from in Odlaw's chapter? Be careful — one is from somewhere else in the book!

ODLAW'S CHECKLIST
Wait, there's more! Look back through the pictures and find . . .

- [ ] Three yellow-and-black-striped top hats
- [ ] A love bird
- [ ] A winking skull-and-crossbones
- [ ] A seagull captain
- [ ] A tunnel traffic controller
- [ ] A man in a bath boat
- [ ] A sleeping dragon
- [ ] A woman in a red beret
- [ ] A monkey on a mast
- [ ] A monster stealing a hat
- [ ] A lightweight boxer

ONE LAST THING . . .
Can you spot Odlaw's binoculars in this section? Only search for them if you dare.

ANSWERS

p. 5 TRAVEL ESSENTIALS
MORE THINGS TO DO

cera rac = race car; dgrna iapno = grand piano; ckhneti snki = kitchen sink

p. 9 PYRAMID PUZZLE

p. 10 WILD AND WACKY W'S

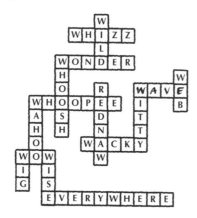

p. 11 BALLOON BEDLAM

MORE THINGS TO DO

The missing pattern is the spots.

p. 12 STARS AND STRIPES

The path marked in yellow leads to Waldo's golden star.

p. 14 TERRIFIC TRAVELS

4 red birds; 7 custard pies; 5 pairs of sunglasses; 9 green hoods; 7 yellow fish; 9 hats with feathers; 8 mustaches.

p. 18 BARE BONES BRAIN BUSTER

1. Odlaw; 2. Blue; 3. Three; 4. A bone;
5. Accordion; 6. Swings and a slide

p. 19 TO THE TAIL END

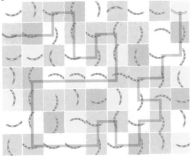

p. 20 WHO'S WHO?

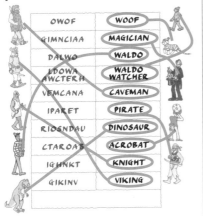

OWOF	WOOF
GIMNCIAA	MAGICIAN
DALWO	WALDO
LDOWA AWCTERH	WALDO WATCHER
VEMCANA	CAVEMAN
IPARET	PIRATE
RIOSNDAU	DINOSAUR
CTAROAB	ACROBAT
IGHNKT	KNIGHT
GIKINV	VIKING

p. 21 WOOF'S WORD WHEEL

1. stone; 2. bone; 3. nose; 4. toes; 5. dog

p. 22 TRUTH OR TAILS?

1. True; 2. False: a dinosaur scientist is called a paleontologist; 3. True;
4. True: TRICERATOPS; 5. True;
6. True; 7. True; 8. False: it had two wings;
9. False: it had a very long neck;
10. False: dinosaurs actually lived until sixty-five *million* years ago. Wow!

ONE MORE THING

Stegosaurus

p. 23 DOG'S DINNER

ON YOUR BARKS, GET SET, GO! MY PALS AND I ARE CHASING OUR FAVORITE THINGS: SAUSAGES, BONES, AND CATS!

p. 28 A COLORFUL TUNE

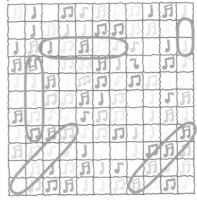

p. 29 BUSY BANDSTAND

drum – sticks; clarinet – reed;
guitar – pick; trombone – mouthpiece;
violin – bow; triangle – rod; piano – keys

p. 32 CAKE-TASTROPHE!

sugar; butter; eggs; flour;
vanilla extract; baking powder

p. 33 CAMERA CLOSE-UPS

1. Wenda; 2. Odlaw; 3. Waldo; 4. Wenda;
5. Wizard Whitebeard; 6. Waldo; 7. Woof

p. 35 DANCING SILHOUETTES

MORE THINGS TO FIND

Wenda's favorite dance is the **waltz**.

p. 36 WOBBLY WORD LADDERS

Here is one possible solution:
HAT, HAY, HEY, KEY
MALT, SALT, SALE, SAME, GAME

p. 39 WORD CASTLE

MORE THINGS TO DO

Open Sesame

p. 40 MIX-UP MADNESS

p. 41 GIANT GAME

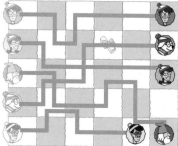

p. 42 SOMETHING FISHY

p. 43 TELEPORTATION TANGLE

p. 44 SHIELDS AND STAVES

p. 45 GENIE-OUS!

p. 47 WHICH WITCH IS WHICH?

p. 52 TOP FIENDS

Warty Gretel | Heave-Ho Henry | Captain Cutlass | Hungry Growler

p. 54 RIDDLING RIDDLES AND TWISTY TONGUE TWISTERS

My hands hang low
But my tail swings high . . .
A: A monkey
I have eight legs and two big eyes . . .
A: An octopus

p. 56 SNAKING WORDS

1. Viking; 2. Musketeer; 3. Skull and crossbones

p. 57 PIRATEY PUZZLE

```
      S E V E N
    S P Y I N G
    S T E R N
    C A P T A I N
P I R A T E S
    B O T T L E
    A N C H O R
E I G H T
```

p. 58 SLIPPERY SEARCH

ONE *VERY* LAST THING . . .

The fun and games aren't over! Can you find a puzzle piece and a pair of dice hidden somewhere in this book? Happy hunting!